for those still searching for true love

THE GLASS
MERMAID

THE GLASS
MERMAID

POPPY LAWLESS

LOVE POTION BOOKS

Love Potion Books, 2015

An imprint of Clockpunk Press

Published by Love Potion Books

PO Box 560367

Rockledge, FL 32956-0367

Cover art by Steph's Cover Design

Editing by Becky Stephens Editing

Book design by Inkstain Interior Book Designing

Text set in Cochin LT.

1 : KATE

THE SURF LAPPED OVER my feet, sea foam tickling my toes. It was early summer, but the lake water was still icy. I closed my eyes and felt the cool waves. In the deep of winter, when the lake would freeze, we always sheltered on one of the small islands that dotted Lake Erie. The humans in those days had called us lumpeguin. Sighing deeply, I opened my eyes and looked down at the rocky shoreline.

"There you are," I whispered, bending to pick up a piece of green beach glass. I lifted it and looked at it in the diming sunlight. It was tear-shaped and worn smooth from its time in the water. A soft white sheen coated the green glass. That made seven green pieces, five light blue pieces, eight white pieces, and seven amber pieces. Not a bad haul. Alas, no red. I rarely found red anymore. The lake had stopped giving up her most beautiful treasures. If I wanted, I could swim down deep to the troves of wave-kissed glass. But I hadn't been below the surface in nearly three hundred years, and I certainly wasn't going to ruin that stretch over some sparkly bauble, even if all my customers begged for red beach glass.

I tucked the green beach glass into my satchel, pulled my long, straw-colored hair back, and then bent to pick up my sandals. I looked out at the lake. The sun was dipping below the horizon. There was nothing more glorious than a Lake Erie sunset. Shimmering shades of rosy pink, orange, and magenta illuminated the sky and reflected on the waves. Breathing in deeply, I tried to inhale the scene. The briny scent of the fresh lake water was perfumed with the lingering smell of snow and flowers. Not for the first time, I wondered what my old home looked like now. Forgotten under the waves, the eerie sea kingdom had been left to be ruled by ghosts and memories.

I sucked in a breath and turned to go. I wouldn't cry. Mermaids' tears were, after all, a special and rare commodity. They carried life itself, and I didn't have much of that magical spark left in me. A single tear could spell my end, sapping out the last of the gift from the deep. No, I'd managed to live for over three hundred years. It wouldn't do to weep over an amazing sunset, a nearly-forgotten past, nor the realization that I was truly alone. It was what it was. I couldn't change the fact that I was the last mermaid.

2 : COOPER

I DIPPED MY BRUSH INTO the purple paint. Not quite the right shade. Swiping my brush in the red, I fattened the color then spread it across the canvas. The sunset was particularly striking tonight. It was a perfect summer sunset, except for the fact that the wind still thought it was early spring. A breeze blew across the lake. It had an icy edge, like it had swept down from some far-off glacier. It chilled my fingers.

I dropped my brush into the jar of water and blew on my hands. For the love of God, would I have to wear gloves in May? I didn't remember Mays in Chancellor being so cold. Maybe all my years in Pensacola, stretched out along those sugar-white beaches, had spoiled me. I loved the water. That's how I'd ended up in Florida in the first place. Marrying my love of people and the sea, my degrees in marine biology and psychology had landed me at the Dolphin Key Sanctuary. I'd made my career doing research on the therapeutic relationship between dolphins and children with disabilities. I'd spent every day in the water until...well, now I was home, back in Chancellor. Lake Erie had been my first love, but she'd grown so cold in my absence.

I blew on my fingers again, picked up the brush, and looked at the fading sunset. I tried to take a mental picture, knowing the colors were about to fade. Too bad, it had been an amazing view. I played the last bit of paint across the canvas then picked up a smaller brush, dipped it in black, and scrawled a number in the bottom: forty-three. This was the forty-third sunset I'd painted. One-hundred forty, give or take, to go.

I leaned back and zipped my coat up to my chin. I told myself I was just taking in the last of the sunset, or letting the pain dry, or stretching my back, then I'd go. But the truth was, I was waiting for her. I shouldn't have been, but I was.

She was strolling up the beach toward me. I'd seen her head out earlier. Like every night, she set off down the beach with her little satchel strung bandolier-style across her curvy body. At first I'd thought she was hunting for shells. It took me almost a week to remember that beach glass washed up on the shores of Lake Erie. She was hunting glass. Every night, she would head down the beach, returning just after sunset. I loved to watch her. It was almost like she melted into the surroundings, her yellow hair the same color as the dried grass, her eyes—the one and only time I'd yet had the courage to look into them—the same dark blue as the waves. Today she was wearing khaki cargo pants, a white T-shirt, and an aquamarine-colored scarf. She was, without a doubt, the most beautiful woman I'd ever seen. But she seemed a little sad, and her sadness helped me stay away. I had no business flirting with women, at least not now, but it was still nice to look at her. And sometimes, when I felt bold, more than look.

Today, I felt bold.

Today, I had something more to say.

While I knew I had no business with her, I couldn't quite get myself to stop looking for ways to break the ice. Today, I found one.

As she neared me, I rose, took a deep breath, and stepped down the beach toward her. "Good evening," I called gently, hoping like hell I wasn't going to annoy her.

She startled a little, like she'd been lost in her thoughts.

Great, scare her to death, moron.

She looked at me with those deep-blue eyes and smiled. "Hello," she said in a voice as soothing as the deep.

3 : KATE

THE PAINTER. ALTHOUGH HE WAS smiling, his awkward stance told me he was nervous. Perhaps me nearly jumping out of my skin had set him on edge. I smiled back at him.

The painter had shown up in Chancellor a little over a month earlier. I'd noticed him one morning as I was headed out to open my shop. My small, A-frame cottage sitting along the beach has wide windows that look out at the water. I'd seen him trudging along with a canvas, easel, and painting kit. It was rare to see anyone walk along the rocky beach outside my house. Pebbly and narrow, it wasn't an ideal place for sun bathing. Almost everyone went to the small, man-made sandy beach at Chancellor Park. I noticed him again and again. Every morning, he would head out with a canvas. Every night, when I went out on my evening walk, he'd be there once again. I tried not to bother him, but I'd snuck a peek of his work. He always painted the fiery sunsets. And in the morning, he would paint the lake and the pastel hues of the sunrise. Sunrises on Lake Erie were not vivid, but they always cast an opalescent sheen on the water. The result was a cloudy mixture of color like the inside of an abalone shell. Beautiful. From what I had seen, the artist's paintings were glorious…almost as glorious as him.

Our exchanges had been little more than polite nods and smiles. I was too hesitant to engage him further even though he was undeniably handsome. He was trim like a cyclist or surfer, his head shaved to a shadow of dark hair, which was usually covered with a cap. He often wore a scarf or a jacket zipped to the top. I guessed him to be a southerner, not acclimatized to Pennsylvania weather. His clear blue eyes were so lovely, but it was his smile that was without compare. It made something dangerous light up in me, something I hadn't felt in a very long time. Despite the danger, I liked the feeling.

"Sorry," I said. "I was a million miles away."

He moved down the beach toward me. I crossed the distance to meet him, hoping I could evoke that smile again. I was relieved he'd finally spoken. We'd had our little routine going on for a month now. I was starting to think that maybe, after all these years, I'd started to lose my mermaid glamour. Most men can't resist the allure that lives inside my skin. In the past, it made living among the humans almost unbearable. But lately, I didn't mind the attention. It felt like my last hurrah. As for the painter, though I would never take anything beyond a simple conversation, it annoyed me that my charms didn't seem to affect him.

"I...I found something I thought you would like," he said hesitantly, holding out his hand. In his palm was a piece of red beach glass. The awkward cut made it look like a jagged heart. It was stunning.

Without thinking, I gently took him by the hand and looked at the glass. I lifted it to admire it in the dimming sunlight.

"Beautiful," I said. "Red is so rare. Where did you find it?"

"On the beach near your boardwalk. Sorry, I know that came out weird. I'm not a stalker or anything. I just happened to notice you outside your house a couple of times."

I smiled reassuringly at him. The last thing he looked like was a stalker. "I must have walked right past it," I said, staring down at the glass. Slowly, I became aware of the fact that I was still holding onto his hand. His skin was ice cold.

"Oh, my gosh, you're freezing. I was just heading back home now. Would you like a coffee? Tea maybe?" What was I doing? Had I lost my mind? I let go of his hand, but then he stuck out his hand to me.

"I'm Cooper," he said.

I smiled. *Introductions first, you lusty mermaid.* "Kate," I said, shaking his hand. Katherine, Kathy, now Kate. It always changed with the fashion of the day. If I stuck around another hundred years, I'd have to go with Katie or Kat. When I'd first come ashore to live among the humans, Katherine was the closest name they had to my real name, Katlilium.

"Thank you for the offer, Kate, but I need to get back," he said with a soft smile, letting go of my hand.

"Oh, okay," I replied, feeling stupid. What was I thinking?

Cooper seemed just as embarrassed as I did. He turned and started packing up his things. Great, now I'd scared him off. Maybe he was married or something. I never even thought to check for a wedding ring. I was getting rusty at this game. That was a good thing. It was a game I had no business playing. I was too old for random flirtations, and had no business falling for anyone with my end so near. Stupid. Feeling awkward, I looked for some way to break the silence.

"May I?" I asked, gesturing to the painting.

"Of course," he replied. He folded his arms across his chest and looked at the painting. "The purple was really something tonight, wasn't it?"

"It reminded me of fuchsias. You've captured it flawlessly." He'd mixed the layers perfectly, even catching the colors reflected along the dark waves and the hint of night sky just at the edge.

"I'm just an amateur," he replied. "But I missed these sunsets." He picked up the canvas, careful not to bump the paint, folded the easel, which he stuck under his arm, then lifted his paint box. We turned and started down the beach.

"Missed? Are you from here?"

He nodded. "My grandma raised me. She's passed on now, but I grew up here. I just came back a month or so ago."

"Oh," I replied, trying to choke down the million or more questions that wanted to come next. "I'm sorry about your grandmother."

"Yeah, lost her about five years ago. Alberta Pearl? Maybe you knew her?"

I nodded. I did know her, when she was about six. "She lived in the little house on Juniper Lane?"

Cooper nodded. "That's the place."

That explained why he was always on my stretch of the beach. There was a walking path through the woods from the end of Juniper Lane to the shore. I smiled at him. "I knew her. Delightful girl," I replied.

In the fifties, she used to come into my soda shop. She always asked for an extra cherry on her sundae. Cheeky little thing with dark hair and clear blue eyes, she was one of my favorite children in town. Like always, I wasn't able to stay in Chancellor too long. People would start to notice how well-kept I was. I'd moved when Alberta was still little and had only been back for the last year myself. When my tenants moved out of the building I owned downtown, I'd decided enough time had passed. All those who could remember me were dead, including little Alberta Pearl. I loved Chancellor. It was the town closest to my home below the waves. I was glad to be back.

"You have a shop downtown, right? The little boutique?" Cooper asked.

I nodded. "The Glass Mermaid."

"That's it. I noticed the sign. I liked your mermaid."

I grinned. If he only knew. "Thank you. I make jewelry," I said then motioned to the red beach glass, "with the glass."

Cooper smiled again. "I'll stop by and have a look."

Having just been turned down for coffee, I wasn't sure what to say. "Sure," I replied.

We reached the boardwalk leading to my house.

"Nice to finally talk to you, Kate. I'll keep an eye out for more beach glass for you."

"Thank you, and thank you for the trinket," I said, still clutching the red glass.

He nodded, his hands full, then smiled and headed back up the beach.

Not wanting to look like a heartbroken teenager, I headed down the boardwalk toward my cabin, pausing just once to glance his direction. To my surprise, he was also glancing back at me. Caught, both of us laughed. I smiled, waved, and then headed into the house.

Once inside, I stared down at the red sea glass...a red heart...a gift from the deep.

4 : KATE

THE BELL ABOVE THE FRONT door of my shop rang when I pushed it open the next morning. The small place, which I'd picked up for a steal during the Great Depression just after the dress shop therein had gone out of business, had a dated charm. A brick beauty constructed during the Victorian era. It boasted high ceilings with elaborate molding, a massive stone fireplace, wood floors, and a glimmering chandelier. After I purchased it, I'd converted it into a soda shop. The glass-lined soda fountain wall and counter was still there. The previous owners had used it as a bookstore. It still carried the sweet scent of old books, many of which I had stored in the back. Now, however, it was my small boutique.

I clicked on the lights. The chandelier sparkled, casting blobs of prismatic rainbows onto the ceiling that I'd painted to look like a cloudy sky. The aquamarine colored walls, trimmed with white molding, reminded me of waves and bubbly sea foam.

Tidying up a display of ships in a bottle, then stopping to breathe deeply beside the handmade soap stand, I headed to the back and turned on the sound system. Moments later, big band music swept through the store. I tapped my fingers along with the music as I sparked up the cash register. I closed my eyes, swaying to the music, remembering a hot summer night long past at the Chancellor Dance Hall and the delicious sailor I'd spent that night with before he shipped out to fight in World Word II. He never came home. From the roaring 20s through the swinging 40s, I must have had what humans call a midlife crisis. I spent twenty odd years running my soda shop in the daytime and doing the jitterbug at night. I'd been a flapper girl. The name always amused me. Some years later, the people of Chancellor started to remark on how young I looked. I left Chancellor. I roamed from town after town along the Great Lakes for nearly thirty years looking for others like me. But I'd never seen a single mermaid or merman anywhere. I finally gave up. There was no one. It was just me. I was glad to be back in Chancellor. When I looked out at the lake, knowing my old underwater kingdom was not so long of a swim away, I felt like I'd come home.

Smiling, I grabbed my duster, and worked my way around the store. When I was done, I headed to my workbench at the back. I set out last night's haul of beach glass on the table, including the red beach glass Cooper had given me. Now, just what was I going to do with that? I snapped on the desk light and slid the pieces of glass under the magnifying lens. I'd given all the pieces of glass a bath after I got home last night, now I just needed to check them. One of the blue pieces had a small flower design on the glass. Probably an old perfume bottle. That piece would sell well. I set it aside.

"Mornin'," a voice called from the door. "Where are you, Katie Bug?"

"Making jewelry," I replied. It was Alice, my friend and the owner of the bagel shop, Hole Lot of Bagels, across the street.

"Moon River," Alice sang loudly and off key as she headed back.

"This isn't Moon River," I called with a laugh.

"How the hell would I know? This is my grandma's kind of music," she replied with a laugh, setting a to-go box and a cup of coffee down in front of me.

"My customers like it."

"Wow, where did you find this?" Alice asked, picking up the red beach glass.

"Well, I —" I began, but Alice interrupted.

"Oh, Kate. Can I have it? Will you make me a necklace? Please? Free coffee the rest of the year!"

"You bring me free coffee almost every day anyway. And no, you can't have it. I wasn't the one who found it."

"Bummer. Commission?" she asked then, looking through the other pieces of glass on my workbench.

"Not quite. The painter gave it to me."

"No. Freaking. Way. You talked to him?"

"Just a little. His name is Cooper. He's from here, I guess."

Alice had moved to Chancellor relatively recently. She'd studied culinary arts at Chancellor College, the small liberal arts college in town, then stayed after she graduated to open her deli and bakery. She wasn't a local. "So, how is he? He looks gorgeous from afar. Is he weird?"

I laughed. "No, he was polite. And he is gorgeous. And he turned me down for coffee, but he did give me this," I said, picking up the red glass.

"Turned you down?"

I nodded.

Alice looked perplexed. "He's gay."

I shook my head. "I don't think so."

"Kate, what man in their right mind would turn you down? *You* have turned down every man in this town."

"I don't know," I said, opening the deli box. I was treated to the scent of a freshly toasted bagel and the ripeness of cream cheese. "There was a vibe there, but he didn't…I don't think he's interested. Probably a good thing. The last thing I need is to get involved with someone." I picked up the bagel and took a bite.

"Well," Alice said with a grin, "you better wipe that cream cheese off your lip just in case."

"In case?"

"In case you're wrong, because your painter is headed this way, and he's carrying something big," she said, gazing out the front window.

5 : COOPER

STUPID, STUPID, STUPID. I CHIDED myself with every step I made as I walked from Juniper Lane toward the shop on Main Street. I'd been doing a good job of lying low since I got back. In spite of my gran's friends' best efforts to get me out socializing, I'd managed to avoid it. Those sweet old gals didn't know, and I had no intention of telling them, why I was keeping to myself. I didn't need a bunch of mother hens checking in on me. As it was, I slept most of the day anyway. The meds always made me nauseous. I hardly needed anyone seeing me throwing up or lying in a sweaty ball of clammy nausea. No one else needed to be dragged into my personal hell.

But if that was the case, if that was how I really felt, why was I walking down Main Street toward The Glass Mermaid?

The wind whipped harshly, pressing against the canvas. I braced myself, holding on tight to the painting. Dammit, why was it so cold? I remembered riding my bike to Frog Creek at this time of year, spending the day swimming, fishing, and catching crawfish. It was May. Why was it so cold in May?

I paused when I came upon the shop. The teal-colored wooden sign hanging over the front door depicted a mermaid holding a heart in her hand. It rocked in the breeze. In the front window was a life-sized mermaid statue. Showing her sense of humor, Kate had put a t-shirt with the saying "I'd rather be a mermaid" on the statue, covering what was probably a clam-shell bra. My thoughts betrayed me for a moment as I remembered the way Kate's white T-shirt had hugged her body, stretching across her large breasts.

Stupid, stupid, stupid, I cursed myself again as I crossed the street, gripping the canvas tightly.

Then I remembered something my gran used to say. "It's not nice to call someone stupid."

Well, okay then, maybe I wasn't stupid, but I surely had no business getting tangled up with this girl. Not now. It's just she looked so taken aback, disappointed even, when I'd turned her down for coffee. It wasn't like I hadn't wanted to go. I did. With every poisoned ounce of me, I did. I just couldn't. But I hadn't meant to hurt her feelings.

The bell over the door rang when I pushed it open. I was greeted with warm, soft light, and the sound of swing music. No way. I loved this kind of music.

"Hi," a dark-haired woman called as she crossed the shop toward me.

I smiled at her. While I didn't know her name, I'd seen her around town. Then I noticed the apron she was wearing. It was dark green with a bagel above the heart. That's where I'd seen her, at the deli across the street.

"Hi," I replied. "Is Kate—"

"She's in the back," the girl said, pushing open the door. "Later, Kater," she called toward the back of the shop.

"See ya," I heard the melodious voice reply. Then, I saw her. Kate smiled as she rose from a small workbench at the back of the store, clicked off a desk lamp, and then came toward me.

I could feel my heart pounding in my chest, and a moment later, a wave of nausea swept over me. Great. Just what I needed. Not now.

"Cooper?" she called.

"Hi, Kate."

"Done already?"

"Done?"

"Your sunrise painting," she answered, then I saw a guilty expression cross her face, like she'd been caught knowing something she shouldn't have.

It made me happy to know she'd noticed me too. "I was out first thing, just did a quick watercolor. I wanted to bring you something," I said then, motioning to the covered canvas. I realized then that this was twice in the last twenty-four hours that I'd brought this woman a gift. No wonder she looked confused when I turned her down for coffee. Maybe I was making a huge mistake. I didn't want to lead her on, I just didn't want her to look sad like that...ever again.

Kate smiled, her dark-blue eyes twinkling in the chandelier light.

I handed the canvas to her.

"For me? Really?"

I nodded.

Carefully, she unwrapped the crinkly brown paper.

"It was in my gran's closet," I said then. "It's not a masterpiece or anything. I painted it during my senior year in high school. Gran always liked the mermaid folktales from this area, used to tell me them as a kid."

Kate's eyes went wide as she studied the painting.

I looked at the canvas. It wasn't a bad painting. It depicted a mermaid sitting in the water, her body half-in and half-out of the water. Her back was to the viewer, letting them look out at the lake with her. I had loved painting the cutaway element, showing the small fish and plants under the water, and the mermaid's tail. From above the surface, she looked like a woman sitting in the water looking out at the lake. What she really was lay beneath.

No, it wasn't a bad painting. I used to paint more when I was younger, back before everyone talked me into pursuing a *real* job. Honestly, I'd just wanted to be a painter. But who can do that these days? This wasn't the Renaissance, and money makes the world go 'round. Maybe if I knew then what I knew now, I would have just followed my bliss. But my years of working with children and dolphins hadn't been for nothing. We'd helped a lot of kids and learned a lot in the process.

"It's stunning," she finally said.

"It's just gathering dust. I thought you might like it for the shop."

"This should be displayed. Cooper, it's so...touching," she said, tears welling in her eyes.

Her joy filled me with so much happiness that for a moment, I forgot everything. I stepped a little closer to the painting...to her. Gently, I set my hand on the small of her back as we looked on. "There are lots of old stories from this area about mermaids. Have you ever heard them? The Native Americans from this area swore mermaids lived in Lake Erie. They called them something else though."

"Lumpeguin." Kate said in almost a whisper.

"That's right, lumpeguin. You've heard the stories then?"

"Yes."

"I painted this for our senior project. We had to paint something relevant to Chancellor. This is actually a cool place, lots of folktales about witches, mermaids, and faerie people. But I was the only one to paint a mermaid...well, a lumpeguin."

"I don't know what to say." Kate said then, and I could see she was truly speechless.

I couldn't help but feel a little pleased with myself. This was the reaction I'd hoped for, whether I wanted to admit it or not.

"So, you like swing music?" I asked.

Kate took a deep breath, shook her head slightly, like she was lost in her thoughts, then said "Sorry?"

"Big band music?"

She giggled a sweet sound like the chiming of a bell. "I love it."

"There is a dance tomorrow night at the old Chancellor Dance Hall. It's mainly for the senior citizens, but my gran's friends have been trying to get me out of the house. I guess they have a swing band. Those old gals, I hate to keep disappointing them. Maybe if I came one time—"

"What time should I be ready?"

"Eight."

"Sounds great."

"It's a date then." The words came flying out of my mouth before I could stop them, and when Kate looked at me, I saw the same startled reflection on her face.

We grinned at one another.

"Thank you again for the painting," Kate said. She carefully set the canvas on the floor, propping it against a display of blown-glass witch balls. She then turned and took my hand in hers. "Really, it's remarkable."

Something desperate stirred in me, and I moved closer to her. I moved my hand from her back to her hip, holding her a bit more firmly. I could feel warmth emanating from her. I looked down at her sweet, petite face. She had wide dark-blue eyes and perfectly-drawn pink lips that looked so soft, so sweet.

Surprising me yet again, Kate put her hand on my shoulder. "Shall we practice? My jitterbug is rusty," she said then turned me, spinning me to the music.

I laughed out loud. Kate giggled. Moving carefully around the displays, we danced. Her face glowed. She had this magic to her. Her sweet, melodious laughter entranced me.

A moment later, the bell over the front door rang, and three older women entered. At the head of the pack, I saw Tootie Row, chief instigator of my gran's old sisterhood.

"Well, well," she said, spotting us. "Now, that's what I like to see!"

I gave Kate a good spin, then smiling, gently let her go. She giggled, covering her mouth with her hand.

"I see you've met Kate," Tootie said.

I nodded.

"She's almost as stubborn as you," the white-haired woman replied.

"Well, you don't have to worry about that anymore," I told Tootie then turned back to Kate. "Tomorrow, then?" I asked her.

"Tomorrow."

I then turned to Tootie who was smiling at me. "There, now you can leave me be." I said, then kissed her on the cheek. I caught her sweet scent of rosewater perfume and cold cream. The smell took me back to my childhood and flooded me with memories of my grandmother.

"Now, that's a good boy," she said. patting my cheek. "Alberta is smiling at you, Cooper."

I grinned. I'd just done the exact thing I'd sworn I wouldn't do, but for some reason, I didn't have the heart to be mad at myself.

6 : KATE

I SPENT THE REST OF the afternoon fighting a war inside myself. As I sat making jewelry and thinking about Cooper, and I couldn't help but smile. It had been a long time since I'd met anyone who lit up a spark inside me. And Cooper, well, just seeing him from a distance had lit up a spark. Watching him walk down the beach every dawn and dusk had made me feel like lightning was shooting through my skin. Now that I'd actually met him, I felt like a bonfire was burning inside me. I hadn't felt anything like it since my first love, Kadan, the merman I'd lost along with everything and everyone else I loved in the black days.

Our life had been simple, peaceful, a respectful accord drawn between the Native Americans and my kind. Then the Europeans arrived. We hid from them. They came and went across Lake Erie for a decade, never knowing what lay beneath the waves. While we kept the peace with the native people, the Europeans did not. It didn't take long for them to start killing one another, and shortly thereafter, war began. It was 1812, and the Europeans had been all over the lake, confiscating our most sacred islands for their own use, sinking ships with their thunderous canons. When winter arrived that year, we found our regular wintering island inhabited by Europeans. We did not speak their language and feared their ways, so we did the only thing we could do. My father, the leader of my people, conferred with the Native Americans who permitted us to live on one of their islands. They knew what we were, but they also knew we meant them no harm. An accord was struck.

In the days leading up to the great lake freeze, however, several of the mers became ill. A strange sickness blackened their fingers and gave them a terrible cough. At the time, I was the strongest and fastest swimmer among my people. My father sent me back to our home below the waves for medicines we knew would ward off the disease. The frigid waters made the swim difficult. By the time I returned to the island, everyone was dead. They had wasted away, their fingers and noses turning black. I found the island riddled with corpses. I was too late. I burned the place, stopping the contamination, then fled to the mainland. In the days that followed, I too took ill. The medicines I carried saved me, and I survived the winter sheltering in a cave. The medicine cured my body, but the sorrow forever wounded my soul. My entire species, including my father, mother, sisters, and my betrothed, Kadan, had died. For many years, I lived with aching guilt. I had the medicine they needed. I just wasn't fast enough to get it to them. Maybe if I'd tried harder, I could have saved them. But I had failed them all.

And now, my time was coming to an end. I could feel it. More and more my body felt...human. The first wrinkles at the corners of my eyes appeared two years before. The magic that lives inside mermaids endures until the end...or until we shed our dying tear. Mermaids' tears carry the spark of life. I must have lost more than five-hundred years of life in the tears I shed for my people. It had taken all my power not to cry the life from me. But I had carried on. And now, my last spark was leaving me. When I was gone, mermaids would truly become what humans thought us to be, nothing more than legend.

Knowing what I did, what business did I have playing around with a man? If I grew to love him, eventually I would have to tell him what I was. That was impossible. And I had no idea how long I had left. A single teardrop could kill me or I might live on another hundred years, slowly aging. How could I explain that?

I had worn my mind out as I thought it over. At five o'clock, I locked up the shop and headed across the street. If there was anything or anyone that could take my mind off my worries, it was Alice.

"A date!" Alice said so loudly that her patrons turned and looked at her.

"Shush," I scolded her.

"Finally. Okay, what are you going to wear?"

"I have no idea. I don't know what I'm doing. Should I go? I don't know."

"Uh, yeah! I mean, he brought you a painting. Who does something like that? That's like the classy version of a mixed tape. Snag him up, girl, or I'll take a run at him."

"Oh, no you won't," I replied. "Besides, what happened to Mr. Fix-it?" I asked, referring to the brawny repairman for whom she kept breaking things so she'd have a chance to win his heart.

"Not interested in me, that's for sure. Nice guy, though. But," Alice said as she sliced open an onion bagel, neatly arranging rolls of salmon-wrapped asparagus beside it in a basket, slathering the bagel with hummus, "the college brought in a new history professor. He's doing some kind of archeology camp this summer. An Indiana Jones, but a ginger, type. Cute. I always had a thing for gingers. I can tell he's a good guy…turkey and pepper jack, red onions, sprouts, and he likes his buns toasted!" she said, gesturing with a little spanking at the end. She stabbed a pickle from the jar with a long fork then gazed at it. "And from what I could see, that package was pretty…" she nodded to the pickle, raising her eyebrows up and down.

"Alice!"

"What?" she asked with mock confusion. She dropped the pickle into the basket beside the bagel and grabbed a cup of her freshly made avocado cream cheese. "Be right back." she said, then headed across the café to serve her customer. She quickly scampered back, grinning, then said, "So, seriously, what are you going to wear?"

"I don't know. The purple dress?"

Alice shook her head. "Too girly."

"I have that gauzy blue one I wore to that wine-tasting you catered."

She shook her head. "You need something with sparkle. You're the glass mermaid. Let your inner mermaid out!" she said jokingly.

Alice had no idea what I really was. If she only knew she'd hit the nail on the head. "Okay, I'll think of something."

I stayed at the café for another couple of hours, getting an earful from Alice. A brief spring rain storm washed through while I was in the café, the rain pounding on the roof in earnest, but it had gone as quickly as it came. Once the rains let up, I headed home. I still wanted to get in my nightly walk, and after a rain storm, there was always more glass on the beach. As well, I hoped I'd see Cooper again. There was still an hour before dark. I had time.

Dropping my bag in the foyer, I rushed upstairs to slip on a pair of shorts and T-shirt before I headed out. The night was turning humid. Finally, summer weather had arrived. I changed quickly. By the time I came out of my room and onto the balcony that overlooked the living room and had a fabulous view of the lake, it had started raining again. Dark clouds rolled across the lake from Canada, obscuring the sunset. Lightning illuminated the black clouds.

Frowning, I scanned the beach. I couldn't see Cooper. Usually I could catch sight of him from the farthest corner of my balcony. He wasn't there. He must have packed it in early because of the rain. A couple of minutes later, large drops splattered against the large windows of the A-frame. Yep, definitely too late. Thunder rolled across the lake.

I headed back to my bedroom and looked it over with assessing eyes. It was painted a soft tan color, almost pink, like a conch shell. I had sepia-hued photos of sailboats on the walls and framed sea stars and shells. My white bed was covered with an unbleached cotton coverlet. All in all, the room looked good, but I should probably change the sheets and tidy up…just in case.

My thoughts surprised me. Just in case of what? In case I brought a man to my bedroom? Yep, that was exactly in case of what. Rather than feeling embarrassed about it, the idea of lying naked with Cooper in my bed thrilled me. I imagined his lean body next to mine. I imagined entwining my fingers in his and feeling his body below me, our flesh pressed against one another.

It had been so long since I'd made love to anyone. Maybe I could allow myself just one last hurrah.

I turned to my closet. Alice was right, time to let my inner mermaid shine. Now, where was that blue sequin dress?

7 : COOPER

I GOT HOME JUST BEFORE the nausea smacked me hard. I should have known from that first wave at The Glass Mermaid that I was in for a rough day, but the events that unfolded thereafter had caught me so off guard that I'd forgotten, for a moment, about my illness.

Once back in Gran's house, however, there was no forgetting. I rushed to the bathroom and unceremoniously threw up my paltry breakfast. But that was just the start of it. I dragged myself to the living room, lay down on Gran's old flower print couch, and barfed up air and stomach acid for the next two hours.

Using every bit of willpower I had, I forced myself into the kitchen to grab a ginger ale and some meds. The doc told me that the nausea would only be bad like this after the chemo, but it wasn't true. It had been more than two months since my last treatment, and the nausea still hadn't gone away.

I sat at the kitchen table sipping the drink and staring at the magnets covering Gran's fridge. As I did so, I was taken back to my childhood, and I suddenly remembered sitting in the exact same spot, looking at the exact same magnets, drinking the same soda, while I listened to my mother retching in the bathroom. Gran had spoken softly, trying to soothe and comfort her. They didn't know it was cancer until my mother was but skin and bones. She was gone just three months after they realized cancer was shredding her pancreas and ripping through her whole body. When I first got sick, I thought it was the flu. I hoped it was the flu. But it lasted too long, and I knew before the doctor had even told me.

"You're young and strong," had been the words that followed the first prognosis. "You'll beat it."

But the words changed as the months passed. "Pancreatic cancer is one of the most aggressive forms of cancer. It'll be a hard fight. You said your mother died from it?"

And then the conversation dissolved into "we can continue the chemo but there isn't much point in torturing your body. It will be a more peaceful end without it...plan on six months."

My mother died when she was thirty. I'd turn thirty-one in June.

I took another sip then headed to bed. Even though my gran was gone, I still couldn't bring myself to sleep in her room. The master bedroom was much larger than the small spare room with its twin bed, but each time I looked into Gran's room, her crocheted coverlet on the bed, her perfume bottles sitting on a dresser filled with her clothes, I didn't have the heart to touch it. I'd leave it like that to remember her. And when I was gone, her friends could sort her things more easily.

Flopping down on the stiff twin bed, I closed my eyes. With a little luck, the medicine would bring me some relief, and I could sleep through the worst of it. As I drifted off, my mind turned to Kate, her laugh, her smile. I'd never really loved a woman my whole life. Now, I finally met someone who made me feel in ways I'd never felt before. But I would be thirty-one next month. Fate had a wicked sense of humor.

I woke up around dinner time, my stomach aching with hunger. The vomiting had cleaned me out, and I'd slept through lunch. I was famished.

When I pushed off my blankets, I discovered it was freezing in the house. I grabbed my sweatshirt then went into the kitchen where I made myself some toast and a cup of tea. From outside, I heard kids laughing. Standing at the sink, I looked out the window above to see three boys in cut-off jean shorts burning down the street on their bikes, fishing poles tucked under their arms like javelins. They were headed toward the path that ran along Frog Creek which emptied out into the lake. I grinned and spooned sugar into my tea. I gazed up at the horizon. It looked like it might rain, but there was still time to get a quick painting done. I'd sworn I would paint every sunrise and sunset, reminding myself to relish each day I had left. Besides, I wanted to catch Kate on her evening walk. Maybe I could find her another piece of beach glass.

I ate my meager meal quickly. While I still felt hungry, I decided not to push my stomach. I headed out with a watercolor pad and simple paint and brush kit stashed in my bag. This would be sunset forty-four. How many more sunsets would I be able to capture before…? I'd given up the hope that I could beat the cancer. It had already spread from my pancreas into my lymph nodes. I was a doomed man. The sunsets and sunrises reminded me that every day was a gift. I just had to remember to cherish what was right in front of me.

Taking the path through the woods, I got to the beach just as the sun was setting. The boys, no doubt up to no good, had ditched their bikes at the end of the path in search of bigger adventures. I smiled, remembering myself in them. I headed down the pebble-lined beach, past Kate's house—no lights were on—to a spot out of the wind just down a ways from her boardwalk.

I pulled out my watercolor pad, paint, and brushes, wetting the paint with some lake water, then got to work. The sky in the distance was dark. Somewhere over Canada, it must have been raining. I pulled out my phone and checked the weather. Sure enough, there were evening storms in the forecast. I'd have to work fast. But more than that, I was disappointed. If it rained, I'd have to wait until tomorrow night to see Kate. Or would I?

Sketching first with my pencil, I drew Kate walking along the beach. I dipped my brush into the yellow, mellowing it with white, and painted her hair. With careful strokes, I recreated her straw-colored tresses. Nagging nausea threatened, but I ignored it, fighting back the waves. I'd forgotten to take another dose of medicine before I left. No doubt I'd pay for it before the night ended. I turned back to the painting. Moving my brush slowly and carefully, I painted the luscious curves of her body, her white T-shirt and tan slacks, working to get her arms and feet just the right shade. I was working so intently on the painting that I was surprised when I heard the first crack of lightning in the distance followed by rolling thunder.

Frowning, I glazed at the horizon. Again, I was wracked by nausea. This time I had to fight back bile as I bent over in terrible pain. Between the weather and my body, I was done for the night. I packed up my supplies, stuffed the painting into a large Ziploc bag, and turned to head back up the beach. When I walked past Kate's house, I saw the lights were still off. I debated, deciding it was probably pushing it too much to show up at her doorstep. I headed down the beach. A few minutes later, rain began to fall.

"Great," I muttered, pulling up my hood. Of course I hadn't thought to bring an umbrella.

I was almost to the forest path when the nausea grabbed me again. This time, however, it was accompanied by a sharp pain that took my breath away. I bent over, tried to breathe deeply, blowing out the pain just like I'd taught the children to do at Dolphin Key Sanctuary. After a moment, the pain resided, and I hurried toward the woods. I had no business out in the rain and no idea what the hell was hurting like that. I needed to get back. I needed to phone the on-call doctor.

I passed the bikes and headed down the small path that would eventually empty out on Juniper Lane. Under the shelter of the trees, the rain let up a bit but the thunder rolled and lightning cracked over the lake. The scents of pine and earth perfumed the air. I tried to breathe in deeply, to calm myself, but a moment later, a terrible pain stabbed my side, stopping me mid-step. Gasping, I leaned against a tree. I knew what would come next. I set down my pack, not wanting to puke all over it, then stepped away and began retching. Tea and toast hurled out of my stomach as a strange pain pierced my side. I gasped loudly as nausea hit me then with a terrible force, making me wretch so hard I fell to my knees. The pink pine needles cushioned my hands as I vomited, my stomach contracting over and over again. The lightning cracked and this time, I felt like it had struck me in the side. Black spots appeared before my eyes, and I crashed onto the ground.

———— ✦ ————

"Mister?" I heard a soft voice call. "Hey, mister, are you all right?"

"Is he dead?" another, more distant voice, asked.

"Shut up, Scott. He's sick or something. Mister?" Someone shook my shoulder.

I opened my eyes a crack. In a haze, I saw three young boys looking down at me. I couldn't answer. I felt like I was drunk, my head swimming, the image of the boys lost in a blur before me.

"Mister, are you okay?" the boy asked again. He was kneeling on the ground beside me.

I tried to open my mouth, but the words wouldn't come out.

"Matt, you got your phone?" the boy at my side called.

"Yeah, my mom made me bring it."

"Call nine-one-one," the boy told him. "Hold on, mister," the boy said softly to me. "Help is on the way."

8 : KATE

I CHECKED MY REFLECTION IN the mirror for what seemed like the hundredth time. I'd put on just enough makeup that I didn't look over-done, but enough to highlight my blue eyes and pink lips. It had been a long time since I had fancied myself up for a night out, even if it was just a night out in Chancellor. I'd tried not to spend the entire day thinking about my date that night. I went to work, ran the store, and closed up without much consequence save Alice's harping on me to look hot. And I hadn't even seen Cooper on the beach that dawn or dusk. I tried to keep my nerves at bay, but that grew increasingly impossible as the day wore on. My stomach was swarming with butterflies as eight o'clock approached. But eight o'clock came and went. I shifted in my dress and checked my cell again. Maybe he thought we were going to meet at the store? But he would have found the store closed. He could have walked back to my house by then. Very stupidly, I hadn't even bothered to ask for his phone number. It was a small town. I figured I knew where to find him if I needed to, but Cooper never struck me as the kind of guy I would need to track down. Maybe I was wrong about that.

I pulled off my heels and flopped down onto my couch, propping my feet on the table.

Stood up, I texted Alice, but I deleted the text before I hit send. It was too humiliating.

Served me right. Looks were deceiving. Surely I knew that better than anyone. Just because he seemed nice, didn't mean he was nice.

I closed my eyes and tipped my head back. To my surprise, the image of Kadan fluttered through my mind. I remembered his blue-green eyes and how his hair would take on honey-colored highlights in the summertime. He always laughed too loud, making my father frown at him. But I loved him and his barrel chest and his big, protective hands. I loved being crushed by his loving embrace. Kadan, the merman whose body I'd burned because the black sickness had taken him, had been the love of my life. Tears threatened. *Careful, Kate.* I was kidding myself. There was no love for me on land. There never had been, and I'd been a fool to let myself daydream. I took a deep breath. If I let myself cry, maybe I could join Kadan and my family. I exhaled deeply. Not yet. I grabbed my cell. It was eight forty-five. I rose and slipped on my sneakers. I might have been a fool for having hope, for letting my heart feel something it shouldn't have for Cooper, but that didn't mean I was going to let him get away with this.

I grabbed my keys, locked my house, and headed toward the beach. Juniper Lane wasn't far.

———∞———

The rocky shoreline crunched under my feet. There was enough moonlight to see where I was going, and I knew the path well. I'd even skipped my evening walk to get ready for the date. It had stormed bad the night before and rained all morning. There was, no doubt, troves of beach glass treasures to be had. The lake always gave up her most precious baubles after a storm, but I'd missed it because I'd been fawning over a man.

I headed down the beach until it met with the path through the woods that emptied out on Juniper Lane. It was a lot darker in the woods than I expected. I pulled out my cell phone. Still no call, no text, no anything. I flipped on the flashlight and headed into the woods. The water in Frog Creek was roaring. The rain last night had been hard and steady, thunder and lightning rolling off the lake. The path was muddy. I flashed my light on the ground. The path was littered with mud puddles. I dodged amongst the trees to miss a puddle but had completely overlooked the root jutting out from the ground. I tripped, barely catching myself against a tree, dropping my cellphone in the process.

"Dammit," I cursed.

My legs were muddy, my dress rumpled, my make-up fading in the humid air. I was angrier than ever. When I got to Cooper's house, I was going to give him a piece of my mind.

I bent to pick up the cell phone but noticed the root I'd tripped on wasn't a root after all. It was a backpack, Cooper's backpack. I scanned the light all around.

"Cooper?" I called.

The creek roared, but I was alone in the little stretch of woods.

I picked up the waterlogged backpack. It must have sat out all night. Maybe I was wrong. The local kids always came here to fish. Maybe the backpack was theirs. Cooper wouldn't just forget his painting satchel in the woods. It seemed unlike him, though I was beginning to doubt I knew him very well anyway. Holding my light with one hand and balancing the pack on my knee with the other, I opened the pack and looked inside. Therein was paint, brushes, a cloth, a small jar, and a watercolor tablet sealed in a Ziploc bag. It was Cooper's pack. I pulled the tablet from the pack, gasping when I saw the image. It was a painting…of me. He had painted me walking along the shore. He'd captured my likeness perfectly.

Okay, now I was really confused.

I stuffed the painting back inside the wet backpack and headed down the lane. I had to dodge through the high grass when I reached the road. The end of Juniper Lane was torn up with large tire ruts. I saw heavy boot prints in the soft, muddy grass leading to and from the woods. Had there been a fishing event? Why had there been so much traffic at the end of Juniper Lane?

I headed around the mud and up the street to the small house that sat on the corner. I remembered seeing Alberta Pearl sitting on the front stoop, her grandmother brushing out her long, dark hair. Alberta's grandmother, Erica, had lived in Chancellor long enough to notice me and how young I always looked. She always eyed me like she knew there was something different about me. There were a lot of women like her in Chancellor, women who had a keen eye for the otherworld. It was no wonder folktales about witches and faerie people abounded in Chancellor.

The lights were off in the old Pearl residence. I walked up the steps, feeling like I was disrupting the ghosts who lingered there, and knocked on the door.

"Cooper?" I called. My anger had simmered down now that it had married with worry. Even if he did decide to stand me up, he wouldn't just leave his paint supplies lying in the woods. Something was wrong.

I knocked again. "Cooper?"

The house was dark and silent, but in the back of my mind, I felt like someone or something was urging me to try the door. Against my better judgment, I did. It was unlocked. Carefully, I opened the door.

"Cooper? It's Kate. Are you home?"

The house was dark. I could hear a grandfather clock ticking inside, but otherwise there was no noise. I looked back. There was a Range Rover SUV parked in the driveway. His vehicle was there, so where was he?

I set the backpack on the floor just inside then turned to go. But still, something nagged at me.

I cast a glance around, pulled off my muddy shoes, and then entered the house, closing the door behind me.

"Cooper?" I called.

There was a small lamp sitting on a table just inside the door. I clicked it on. It illuminated the kitchen wherein I saw row after row of medicine bottles sitting on the window ledge. Had Alberta been so sick? I peered around the corner into the living room.

"It's Kate. Cooper, are you here?"

Nothing. But what I saw next surprised me. In the living room, the walls were completely covered with paintings. Sunsets on Lake Erie were always so vivid, and he'd caught their fire. All around the room were paintings, big and small, of the lakeshore at sunrise and sunset. As I looked over the images, I noticed something. There, again and again, he had painted…me. I appeared in no less than ten of the paintings. All the while I'd been watching him, he'd been watching me, working me into the sunsets. Sometimes he'd painted me as a silhouette. Sometimes he painted me bending to pick up beach glass. He caught me in the red dress I'd worn to a Chamber of Commerce charity fundraiser. I'd walked home from the event along the beach that night, my heels dangling in my fingers. As I studied the paintings, I realized that each was numbered. He'd painted more than forty, others still sitting on the floor to be hung.

My eyes scanned the walls. He'd catalogued every day. Why?

My anger subsided and turned to anxiety. Where was he?

I headed back into the kitchen, stopping to take a notepaper from the refrigerator which was covered in magnets. From animals, to fruit, to commemorative spoons, to framed pictures, there was barely a bare inch on the appliance. I pulled the little pen from the refrigerator notepad and started writing, telling him I'd found his pack, when a photo on the refrigerator caught my attention. It was a faded image of a woman in her twenties. At first I thought it was Alberta, but this woman's hair was much redder. The image was in a little frame held by two angels. The banner underneath said "In Loving Memory" with the word "Daughter" hand-painted in gold above the image. Alberta's daughter? Would that make her Cooper's mother?

I stared at the woman looking out from the picture. The photo had been taken on Christmas. There was a Christmas tree in the background. Digging under that tree was a smiling child holding a wrapped gift. His mother then. Human lives were so fragile. I pitied Cooper. Loosing someone before you were ready was never easy. To lose a mother...well, I'd had that experience myself. Your life is never the same thereafter. It's like the compass of your life is forever lost.

Leaving my number at the bottom, I finished the note, stuck the little pen back where I'd found it, and headed back outside.

My muddy sneakers were wet and cold. I closed the door tight behind me, uncertain if I should lock up the house or not. I didn't want to lock him out of his own home. Feeling confused and worried, all my anger swept away, I headed home. Wherever Cooper was, I hoped he was okay.

9 : COOPER

THE AMBULANCE WAILED AS IT pulled away from Juniper Lane. People I didn't know leaned into my face and asked my name. I managed to whisper out "Cooper McGuire" and "cancer" before I faded once more.

The *beep, beep, beep* sound on a machine woke me sometime later. I didn't even have to open my eyes to realize I was in the hospital. The smell gave it away. There was nothing worse than the smell of the hospital with its lingering odor of disinfectant, bodies, and fluids. I opened my eyes slowly. It was dark outside. There was a window beside my bed. The stars were twinkling in the night's sky. Had I only been out for a few hours?

My skin felt itchy. They'd put in an IV. My face was damp where the oxygen mask pressed against my cheeks. I pulled it off causing a monitor to bong. I coughed heavily then sat up. In the very least, I had the room to myself. And like every hospital, this one was cold. My feet felt like they were sitting in a bucket of ice water.

"Mister McGuire," a nurse said then. "Nice to see you awake. Let's check your blood pressure, shall we?" The nurse pressed a button on the wall, silencing the alarm, then unhooked the oxygen mask and stowed it.

"Which hospital is this?"

"Titus Medical," she replied. "You're in the ICU. You gave us quite the scare."

"Doctor Archer?"

"He was by to see you this morning. I expect he'll be back later this evening," she said as she wrapped my arm with the band and began checking my blood pressure.

"This morning? How long have I been here?" I asked. I'd missed my date with Kate. She probably thought I stood her up.

The nurse silenced me, putting one finger to her mouth, as she counted. After a moment, she let the air out of the band and made a note on my chart. "You came in last night," she said then carefully put her stethoscope down the front of my hospital gown, pressing the cold metal against my chest.

I stayed still and waited. There wasn't anything new she could to tell me. I knew what had brought me there. Now I just wanted to go home. There wasn't anything they could do for me. Why did this have to happen now? I just wanted one night, one last night with a beautiful woman. I wanted just one night to pretend I wasn't a dead man walking, to imagine what it would be like to fall in love with someone like Kate, to touch her skin, maybe even kiss her. I wanted just one night to imagine what it would be like to have a life and children and a wife. I couldn't even have that.

"All right, Mister McGuire," she said, then sat down on the side of my bed and made a note in my chart.

"What did Doctor Archer say?" I asked. "I want to go home."

The nurse nodded then turned and smiled at me. Her expression was soft. I could see in her eyes she knew. "I can't let you go until Doctor Archer gives us the say so. He wants to double check your medications, see what he can do to make you more comfortable. A hospice worker was by earlier. I think they're still here if you'd like me—"

"No. I just want to go home. And my cell phone. Is my cell here?"

The nurse nodded then opened a drawer on the bed table beside me. Inside was my watch, keys, and cell. She handed it to me.

I punched the button, but the battery had gone dead.

"I have that same phone. You want me to bring my charger?" she asked me.

"No," I said, closing my eyes. I didn't even have Kate's phone number and it was too late to call her at the store. Even if I did, what would I tell her? That I was at the hospital? Then I'd have to explain everything to her. Maybe it was better this way.

"Okay, then. I'll let you sleep. Can we call anyone for you, hun? There wasn't anyone listed in your records."

"No. Thank you."

Without another word, the nurse left. I lay there listening to the monitor beep. Maybe it would be better if it ended soon. The waiting, the false hope, was more than I could take. And now my illness, which caused my absence, had no doubt hurt Kate, just as I knew it would. My first instinct was right. I needed to leave her alone.

10 : KATE

"WHAT DO YOU MEAN HE didn't show up?" Alice asked as she set my dinner down in front of me with a clunk. I'd managed to dodge her that morning. Her Indiana Jones had brought his archeology campers to the deli for breakfast, much to my great relief, so I got away with simply saying "we'll talk later." Now, however, I was in for a drilling.

"Hey, watch my bagel!" I said jokingly as the top of my bagel slid toward the table.

"Sorry. He didn't call or anything?"

"No, but it was weird…"

"Weird? What do you mean, weird?"

"Well," I began, realizing how bad it made me sound. "I walked over to his house," I said. Alice raised an eyebrow at me. "I was mad, all right. I didn't even know what I was going to say, but I was just so confused...and annoyed...but mostly confused. Anyway, I walked along the shore and through the woods to Juniper Lane, and I found his bag in the woods. It was soaking wet, like it sat out all night.

"Maybe he just forgot it?"

I shook my head. "He had his paint supplies inside."

"Okay, that is weird."

"When I got to his house, it was unlocked. His SUV iss there. His house was dark. I drove by this morning, and his lights were still off. Maybe I should call the police."

"Maybe he went out of town with friends. But why wouldn't he lock up?"

I nodded. "Exactly. I don't know what to do."

The door above the bell rang. Tootie Row and her husband Milt came in, her husband promptly taking a seat by the front door while Tootie headed toward the counter where I was sitting.

"One sec," Alice said then turned to Tootie. "All ready!" Alice lifted a massive bag full of bagels.

"Good girl. Did you pack the extra honey pecan spread?"

"Of course," Alice replied as she started punching keys on her cash register.

"My relatives come in tomorrow morning. They always cry for your bagels, honey."

"They have good taste," Alice answered.

Tootie laughed as she dug into her purse for her wallet, but then she saw me sitting at the counter.

"Oh, Kate," she said, gently setting her hand on my shoulder. "How is Cooper? I didn't get a chance to go by. I'm just so busy preparing for my sister and her grandkids. What happened? Did they say?"

"I'm sorry, what?"

"Oh," Tootie breathed in surprise. "You don't know?"

Confused, I shook my head.

"Rose's grandson, Scott, was out with some other boys at Frog Creek yesterday evening, and they found Cooper passed out in the woods! They called an ambulance to take him to Titus Medical. I thought for sure someone would let you know."

I rose and picked up my purse. "No...I...I had no idea." I felt like someone had poured ice water down my back. "I've got to go," I told Alice.

She nodded. "Call me."

"Wish him well for me," Tootie said then turned to Alice. "You know that boy's mother died of cancer. I hope it's nothing serious."

Her words rung in my ears as I thought about all those bottles of medicine sitting on the window sill. With my hands shaking, I rushed out of the deli. It had never even occurred to me that maybe something terrible had happened to him. He'd gotten sick. And I...I hadn't been there for him.

I rushed down Main Street, turning onto Fence Post Lane which led to the public dock. I was planning to just jump onto the beach and rush home. I could make it to Titus Medical in twenty minutes if I hurried. I was surprised, however, when I turned the corner. At the end of the dock several TV crews had gathered around a man with curly red hair. He was holding something in his hands. I could hear a reporter asking him questions. Bright light glared on his face. Nearby, a group of college students—evident from their Chancellor College sweatshirts—stood watching in awe.

"There was anecdotal evidence, folklore, that the Native Americans inhabited the islands in Lake Erie, but physical evidence has been hard to come by...until now."

"Why do you think these artifacts have been overlooked for so long?" a reporter asked as I moved toward the crowd, a sick feeling rocking my stomach.

"Mainly because it was small and covered in scrub. Archeological digs have been completed on other larger islands with limited success, mainly unearthing evidence of European use of the islands. While we've long-suspected we'd find artifacts on the smaller islands, we never expected anything of this scale. Earlier this spring, a fisherman discovered artifacts on the island's bank. That got our attention. Since the college recently acquired the island, the board thought it wise to do a thorough investigation. What we found today, however, was unimaginable."

"How many remains were discovered?"

"We've only uncovered the first few, but sonar readings suggest there are nearly one hundred. The bodies were laid out in ceremonial fashion before they were burned."

"Was it a slaughter? Sacrifice?"

The man shook his head. "No, they were burned after death. You can see from the scorching on this skull," he said, lifting a charred skull.

My knees went weak as I gazed into the empty sockets of the skull he held up. It stared back at me, watching me, accusing me. On a TV screen nearby, they were displaying a map of Lake Erie, pinpointing the island where the archeologist had made this discovery. The island...the island where my kind had died...the skull he was holding had belonged to one of my people.

The reporter then turned to a young woman standing near the archeologist. The reporter asked her a question, but in my haze, I missed it.

"You just don't see this kind of craftsmanship amongst the Native Americans," the young woman said, holding something in the palm of her hand. "It was on one of the bodies. It's extremely rare to see such metallurgy and jewel work. It looks Viking," she said then lifted a charred band. It was a bracelet. "You can't see it well, but there is agate and amber worked into the band," the girl said proudly.

The reporter smiled then turned to the camera. "Quite a find for these junior archeologists. We'll bring you further updates on this remarkable discovery as they become available. Back to you, Tom."

"Cut," someone called, then the lights went dim.

I stood in the darkness, the stars twinkling overhead. The crowd cheered the students and professor for their discovery. My family, my friends, my Kadan. I took a step toward the crowd. What would—

what *could*—I say? This was sacrilege. They would go there and dig up the ghosts that haunted me. What would they find in the remains? What other clues that the bodies lying in the mud were Native Americans would the clever young archeologist uncover? She looked at the bracelet, her eyes full of wonder. I wondered how she would feel if I told her that I was the one who'd made it. It had been a gift for my sister, Merlilium, whose diseased body I'd burned after gently crossing her hands on her chest, adjusting the bracelet so it shimmered in the sunlight. It amazed me to think the bracelet had withstood the fire, but that was the gift of mer metalworking, ores mined from the deep and crafted with skill. My kind had once been masters of the craft.

I stood in the darkness and debated. My past had collided with the present. Would the bodies yield the secrets of the deep? Did I have a duty to protect them? If so, what could I do? But more so, my mind bent on the here and now. Cooper was in the hospital. He was real and alive and near as I could tell, alone.

I took a deep breath and turned down the beach.

11 : COOPER

"ARE YOU CERTAIN, COOPER? I can admit you to residential care. You'd have someone with you twenty-four hours a day. In the very least, let us arrange for hospice to visit you. There is a very good, supportive team of people in Chancellor," Doctor Asher said.

I lay in the hospital bed staring at the television. The local news had just aired a report of archeological finds on an island in Lake Erie just off the coast from Chancellor. When I was a child, I'd found a cave in the cliff side down shore. Within, there had been evidence that the place had been inhabited long ago. There were paintings on the walls of the cave, spirals and images of creatures that looked something like mermaids...no, lumpeguin, as Kate had called them. I clicked off the TV.

"No residential care," I said.

"The hospice? Please? For me?"

"Fine."

"I'll have the nurses draw up some papers before you go," Doctor Asher said then paused. "It's time to start being careful," he said, setting his hand on mine. His blue eyes looked sorrowfully at me. He shook his head. "It's coming," he whispered. "Your white blood cell count is dangerously low. Stay close to home. Start saying your good-byes."

To whom? I wondered, but the image of Kate laughing, her golden hair shimmering, danced through my mind.

"Go ahead and get dressed. They'll bring you up a wheelchair. Someone at the nurses' station already called you a taxi."

"Thank you."

Doctor Asher shook his head. "Are you certain about the DNR?" he asked, looking down at the papers I'd signed. If I stopped breathing, if my heart stopped, it would be over. I didn't want to prolong my body's torture.

"Yes," I said absently then gazed out the window. The moon was a sliver in the sky. How beautiful it looked against the dark blue tapestry of the night.

Doctor Asher nodded. "Please call the on-call number if you need anything."

"I will. Thank you, doctor."

He nodded slowly then stopped at the door. He turned back and looked at me. "Good-bye, Cooper."

I smiled at him. "Good-bye, doctor. Thank you for everything."

He inclined his head then left.

"And they put broccoli in the goulash, can you believe that? They called it primavera something or other. Nasty," a chatty nurse's aide was saying as she pushed me to the curb where the taxi waited. Taking me by the arm, like I was some kind of invalid, she helped me into the taxi. "Have a great night," she called, slamming the door shut behind me.

I sat in silence as the diver guided the car into the night. Titus Medical was located in the business district of the nearby town of Waterville. Chancellor was just a short drive away.

The cab driver, sensing I was in no mood to talk, kept his eyes on the road and his mouth shut as we drove toward the lakeshore. The land surrounding Chancellor was covered in vineyards. There was a microclimate formed by lake-effect weather that created the perfect condition for growing grapes. The Chancellor wine industry was huge. The college even had a program in their culinary department for future wine-makers, funded by the Moore family and their massive estate, the Blushing Grape vineyards. In the autumn, when the grapes were ripe for harvest, the air all around Chancellor was perfumed with the smell of grapes. I had missed that smell, missed autumn in Chancellor. Now, it seemed, I would never see another fall.

I closed my eyes and tipped my head back against the seat. I had gone through all the stages they said I would experience...the grief, the rage, the denial, and now, the begrudged acceptance. Just because I'd accepted my end was coming didn't mean I liked it. I would never have a wife. I would never have children. There would never be another person from my family to live on Juniper Lane. I was the last of us. And my time was nearly done.

A tear slid down my cheek.

I didn't want to die.

THE GLASS MERMAID

I fumbled with my keys a few minutes only to discover that I'd actually left my house unlocked. Thankfully, Chancellor was a relatively safe town. When I clicked on the lights, I was surprised to see my backpack sitting inside the door. How had that gotten there?

Everything was just as I left it, my amber-colored medicine bottles lining the window ledge, my water cup sitting beside the oven. But then I noticed a piece of paper lying on the table. I sat down and picked it up. It was a note from Kate.

My hand trembled as I read it. I could only imagine the pain and frustration I had caused her when I hadn't shown up. Clearly, she'd come by the house to see if I was there. Was she the one who'd left the backpack? Had she walked down the beach looking for me?

I crushed the note in my hand and pressed it against my forehead. My whole body shook with frustration. Such a beautiful woman, such a lovely spirit living inside her, and I had hurt her. I knew better. I'd just wanted something I couldn't have.

I lay my head down on my arms and wept.

12 : KATE

I COUNTED THE ROOM NUMBERS as I walked down the hallway of the ICU. Twelve, eleven, ten, nine…there was eight. I took a deep breath and entered the room slowly, quietly, to find…no one.

"Oh, sorry, hun," an aide told me as she stripped down the bed. "Are you looking for Mister McGuire?"

Was I? I didn't even know his family name. His grandmother was a Pearl, but Cooper would have his father's name. I didn't even know what it was. "Cooper…"

"I took him down to the taxi a while ago," she said then whispered, "the nurses are running behind tonight, slow about finishing up his discharge papers. They should have told you he'd already left." She was about to say more but stopped abruptly when someone entered the room behind me.

"He's gone already?" a woman.

"Sure is," the aide said.

"But he's still in the system. God, they're so slow processing paperwork," the woman behind me grumbled.

"Uh-huh," the aide said in a know-it-all tone as she pulled the sheets off the bed.

"Are you a family member?" the woman asked me.

Feeling like my mind was pulling in a million different directions, I turned and looked at her. "Sorry?"

"Mister McGuire, are you a relative of his?"

I shook my head. "N-no, we're friends."

The woman tapped a manila envelope in the palm of her hand as she considered. "Well," she said, looking at the envelope, "he was supposed to have these before he left. Seems like someone fouled up somewhere. I could mail them, but he should have them sooner. Will you be seeing him tomorrow? I know it's late now."

"I can take them to him," I said. I didn't know what was going on, but I knew I wasn't angry anymore. All I wanted was to see Cooper, to make sure he was all right.

"It's not exactly protocol," the woman said then, "but you promise you'll get it to him?"

I nodded.

"You didn't hear that, Deloris," the woman said to the aide.

"Hear what, hun?"

The woman smiled. "Thank you," she said, then handed the envelope to me and turned and walked away.

I looked at the return address. It was stamped with an address for the local hospice.

"Have a good night," I called to the aide.

"You too," she called.

I turned and exited the room, clutching the envelope tightly against my chest. I walked down the narrow halls of the hospital, feeling like a zombie, and rode the elevator back to the ground floor. I slid into the driver's seat of my car, closing the door behind me. I stared at the envelope. It wasn't sealed. Mermaids were inherently curious, but something deeper drove me. I needed to know.

I opened the envelope.

Inside, I saw Cooper's name assigned to a hospice worker and details documenting the care he could expect in the coming days.

I wasn't the only one who was dying.

I pulled my car into my driveway and clicked off the lights. It was three o'clock in the morning. Cooper would be sleeping. I left the envelope on the seat of my car and headed down the boardwalk to the beach.

There, the lake waters lapped lazily against the shoreline. I gazed up at the moon. It hung in the sky like a gem. I pulled off my clothes. I felt detached from my movements. It was like I was watching myself from above. I took everything off and walked, naked, to the shoreline. I didn't pause like I usually did, to let the waves kiss my toes and nothing more, but I pressed into the water. The lake was cool. I pressed forward until the waves engulfed me up to my chin. It had been nearly three hundred years since I'd transformed into what I truly was.

I dunked my head below the waves and felt the lake embrace me. It enveloped my hair, my ears, hugging me like a long-lost friend. I swam, stretching out my arms in the cool water, kicking my legs. A little more. A little more. Underwater, I opened my eyes, letting my human vision, which saw only the darkness of the deep, fade away. Slowly, my eyesight reformed into the vision of a mermaid's. Light and color flashed so brightly that it nearly startled me. The black water crystalized into a haze of color and light. The massive lake fish swam close to me, curious to find me below the waves. The iridescent colors of their scales shimmered like rainbows.

I opened my mouth and inhaled deeply, letting the lake water filter into my lungs and with it, the oxygen that was the breath of life. The small gills behind my ears opened, and I inhaled and exhaled the water, becoming one with the lake once more.

I turned in the water then and looked at my legs. Kicking the long limbs one last time, I closed my eyes and felt the swirl of mana magic surround me. A soft caress, like my legs had been wound with a scarf, enveloped me. My legs tingled, a prickly—but not painful—feeling like electricity flooded the lower half of my body.

When I opened my eyes again, my legs were gone. In their place was my emerald-colored tail, the tips trimmed with glimmering gold.

I laughed, the sound bubbling upward. Overhead, the stars and glimmering moon looked distorted against the water's surface, casting long shimmering streaks of silver. Wondrous.

I opened my arms wide, feeling the water surround me, then turned and dove deep, searching for the lake bottom. I'd forgotten how fast I was, my tail pushing me powerfully forward, driving me through the waves. I swam over rises and around boulders. I spotted a sunken ship in the distance, a remnant of the great war between the Europeans, now covered in algae and zebra mussels. I swam deep, the bottom of the lake calling me. There, long fingers of tall seaweed grew from the bottom of the lake. I darted around them, laughing as I passed a massive old turtle who looked surprised to see me. They, like us, had lives that spanned decades. Did he remember my kind? Was I the first mermaid he'd seen in years?

I swam toward the rocky crevice that ran just north of Chancellor. As I moved along, I saw the crevice was full of beach glass. Hundreds of shimmering pieces lay there waiting to be tossed up and washed to the rocky shoreline. There were heaps of pieces, blues, greens, purples, ambers, white, and more red than a jewelry maker could ever dream of. I swished my tail hard and passed it by, pushing out deeper into the lake, gliding toward the surface. I leapt out of the water, catapulted by my long tail. I danced with the waves, diving in and out of the water, as I moved quickly toward my destination.

It didn't take me long to reach the island. As I neared the shore I slowed and looked, being careful to keep my body hidden under the waves. The island was quiet. It was clear that people had been there. The college had posted a sign at the head of the island declaring it theirs. There was some sort of plastic equipment shed near the sign. The brush had been mowed low. I circled the island, looking for any sign or sound of humans, but there was nothing.

Slowly, I swam toward shore. I stopped when my tail touched the rocky bottom of the lake then closed my eyes, willing myself back to human form. Again, I was treated with that same warm feeling. It didn't take long before I felt the swish of water between my legs.

Having been human for so long, I was conscious of the fact that I was naked as I walked toward the shore. I hoped the professor and his crew hadn't decided to camp out all night. They'd be in for quite a sight...and Alice would no doubt accuse me of throwing myself at her new mark. But there was no boat. There was no one.

When I reached the shoreline, I had to pause. It was the same place, but so many years had passed. The trees were taller, the banks eroded from so many hard winters. Taking a deep breath, I crossed the shore and walked up the narrow slope onto the island. A path to the old settlement had been cleared. It amused me to think that the scientists were following the exact path we'd used. It was almost like the island had told them where to go. I followed the path to its end.

The excavation site had been marked off. Moonlight cast enough glow that I could see opened graves which were covered with a tarp. The wind whipped across the island, chilling my skin as my wet hair dripped down my back. Shivering, I walked over to the unearthed grave and pulled the tarp back. They had uncovered two bodies.

From the way the arms were arranged, I recognized Merlilium's body at once, her bracelet taken from her. To her side was the body of an orphaned mermaid, Kisla, who'd adored my sister. I'd laid her to rest at my sister's side, wanting her to go into the afterlife with someone she loved. Still buried, on the other side of my sister, was Kadan.

Grief wracked me, and I fell to my knees. Tears threatened, but I drowned them. A terrible moan escaped my lips. It echoed into the night's sky. I lay down on the earth, pressing my cheek against the dirt, imagining I was lying once more in my Kadan's arms. I was supposed to die with them. I'd been meant to die with them. I shouldn't have lived. I shouldn't have survived. I dug my hands into the earth, clutching soil and grass as I moaned in heart-wrenching agony. I could die right then. I could end it all, let the last tear fall, let the spark of life leave me. I opened my eyes and at my sister's skeleton. She was my younger sister, taken before she'd ever loved, or had children, or had even lived a life...much like Cooper.

I closed my eyes and listened to the waves lap onto the shore. I didn't want to live anymore. I didn't belong to this world. My world was long forgotten. With certainty in my heart, I knew it was time to end it.

But there was one thing I needed to do first.

I turned and kissed the earth, kissing my Kadan, then rose.

Walking back to the shore. I dove under the waves and headed toward Chancellor.

13 : COOPER

A KNOCK ON THE DOOR woke me. I hadn't even bothered to crawl into bed. I'd crashed on Gran's couch, too miserable to move. When I opened my eyes, waves of nausea hit me.

There was a knock on the door again.

I inhaled deeply, trying to push the sickness back inside me. It wasn't even dawn yet. Who in the world would be knocking on my door?

Rising on wobbling knees, I went to the door. In the dim light, I saw the silhouette of a woman standing there. I opened the door.

"Kate?" Her hair was dripping wet and she had an envelope clenched in her hand. She pushed the envelope toward me.

"I went to the hospital…" she began then paused. When she looked at me, the light in the kitchen caught the deep sapphire hues in her eyes. She looked sad. No, she looked something beyond sad. She had the strangest expression on her face. She looked at the envelope.

I took it from her, seeing the name of the hospice on the envelope. I slid the papers out, seeing what she, no doubt, had already discovered.

"Will you come with me?" she asked.

"You're all wet," I stammered.

She smiled, dug into her pocket, and pulled out something, handing it to me.

I opened my hand.

Placing her hand in mine, she set something in my palm.

I opened my hand to see that it was filled with red beach glass. "I thought you said it was rare," I stammered stupidly.

"Not if you know where to look."

I set the envelope and beach glass on the table. I turned to grab my jacket, but the nausea wracked me. Uncontrollably, I rushed to throw up into the sink. My hands clutched the side of the white porcelain basin as I wretched over and over again. If I hadn't felt so miserable, I probably would have died from embarrassment.

With my eyes closed, I heard the refrigerator door open followed by a snap as she opened a can of soda. I then heard the cupboard.

"Here," she said, after my vomiting had subsided.

I opened my eyes to see her standing with a glass of ginger ale in one hand and a napkin in the other. I took the soda from her and sipped slowly, wiping my mouth.

"Will any of these help?" she asked, picking up the medicine bottles.

I pointed to the one on the end.

She handed it to me.

She wore a very strange, almost serene, expression on her face. What in the world was going on with her?

"Kate?" I asked, raising an eyebrow.

She motioned to the bottle.

I took two pills, swallowed, and washed it down with the soda. There was a small bottle of mouthwash sitting beside the sink. I picked it up and cleaned my mouth. How humiliating. I turned and smiled abashedly at her.

Kate nodded affirmatively then reached out for me.

I slipped on my boots and followed her outside.

It was still dark outside, but you could feel dawn on the horizon. Taking my hand in hers, she led me through the woods toward the shore.

"Where are we going?" I asked.

"To the lake."

"Why?"

"For the sunrise."

"Kate?"

"No questions, Cooper," she said, squeezing my hand.

She led us through the dark and soon we emerged on the rocky shoreline. With my stomach empty, the medicine worked fast, dispelling my nausea. But still, my body felt weak and pain lingered in my stomach. My organs were beginning to fail. My end was nearly here. I could feel it.

When we reached the lakeshore, we stood hand-in-hand looking out at the water. Kate eyed the horizon, her blue eyes wide, then she turned and smiled at me. Standing with her back facing the lake, she then did something very unexpected. Kate pulled off her white T-shirt, revealing her full, naked breasts. She then slid off her shorts to reveal she was naked underneath. I looked away.

"Don't," she said. "Look at me. All of me," she whispered.

Turning back, I let my eyes slide down her beautiful body. She was perfect, large breasts above a trim waist, her legs and arms athletic. I let my eyes slide down her waist, down below her bellybutton, to her secret feminine parts. She was so beautiful.

"Now you," she said.

"Me?" For a brief moment, a flicker of embarrassment flashed through my mind. I was already aroused. What would she think about that? But then I realized, if she was that brave, then I had to be brave too.

I pulled off my clothes, feeling the cold air surrounding me. It nipped horribly at my ears and toes. When I pulled down my jeans, then my boxers, I felt shy for a moment. But then I saw Kate's large eyes on me, smiling, that strange wistful expression on her face as if she were holding back tears.

"Let's go," she said then, grabbing my hand, pulling me toward the water.

"But…but its freezing," I protested.

"What's the worst that can happen?" she asked.

The sharp poignancy of her reply wasn't lost on me.

"Come on," she said then led me into the water, splashing me as I followed after her.

I couldn't help but laugh in spite of myself. I chased her into the waves, feeling nothing but joy. She kicked water at me, laughing and squealing as I grabbed her, tumbling us both into the water.

Without thinking, I pressed my mouth against hers. I swooned as I felt a dizzying sensation. Her warm lips pressed against mine. I held her wet, naked skin, feeling her warmth as she leaned against me. I felt her heart beating quickly and the grit of sand on her fingers as she ran her hand across my back. A moment later, however, she pulled away.

"Come on," she said, then dove under the waves. I watched the water where she disappeared then saw a strange golden light.

"Kate?" I said, stepping forward into the chest-high water. She didn't come back to the surface. Light glimmered under the waves. It seemed to move like it was alive. "Kate?" I called again. The light moved toward me, and a moment later, Kate broke the surface of the water, her head and neck just above the waves.

"The sun is about to come up," she said as she looked over my shoulder toward land. "Will you carry me to shore?"

"Carry you?" Was she hurt? Surely she knew I was in no condition to carry anyone.

She nodded then swam toward me, that golden light trailing behind her. She put her arms around my neck then pressed her body against me. When she did, something felt odd, but warm and soft like silk.

"Carry me," she whispered again.

I reached under the water and slid my hand down her back but something felt strange.

Kate giggled.

"What? What is this?" I asked as I slowly made my way back toward shore. As I did so, the golden light around Kate began to glow brighter and brighter and soon I could see what felt so different. "Kate," I whispered aghast as I stared down at the bundle in my arms. I had gone into the lake with the loveliest woman I'd ever met in my life, but was returning to shore with…a mermaid.

"Take me to shore, please," she whispered.

I looked at the horizon. The sky was illuminated gray with the first edges of pink lining the skyline. What I was seeing was a miracle. I was being shown a miracle.

I carried the lovely creature in my arms and set her down on the shoreline beside me. Her long emerald-colored tail stretched out on the shore. I stared at her in amazement.

Kate reached out, took me by the chin, and then kissed me lightly. Then she gently lay me down beside her.

"I've walked the Earth for nearly three hundred years," she whispered then, pausing to kiss me on my forehead. "But I never felt love for any human until I set eyes on you. There is a spirit inside you that deserves to live, a goodness in you that is coming to an end too soon. I can't let that happen," she said, then looked off at the horizon. Sunlight shimmered from land out onto the lake. When Kate turned and looked back at me, an enormous tear was streaming down her cheek. The tear glistened with golden light.

"Live," she whispered, then gently wiped the tear from her cheek with the tip of her finger. She danced her wet fingertip across my lips. "Live," she whispered again, pressing her lips against mine, then she went still, slumping onto my chest.

To my amazed eyes, I watched as the golden light transformed her tail back into legs. But the glow didn't stop there. It moved onto me, covering my whole body. It was like I'd been submerged in a bath of love and light. My whole body glimmered as I was filled with the sensations of warmth and healing. I heard my heart beating. I felt my blood pumping through my veins. I breathed deeply, feeling my lungs take in the shimmering glow. When I exhaled, I could feel the darkness and illness and death leaving me. My body felt clean, renewed.

As the sun rose, filling the world with light, I knew my cancer was gone.

And the mermaid who'd given me the precious gift of life lay unmoving against my chest.

EPILOGUE

THE SOUND OF SWING MUSIC filled the little house on Juniper Lane.

"Daddy," my littlest daughter, Kayla, called from the yard. "Turn the sprinkler on."

"I'm coming," I called. I pushed open the door only to get smacked square in the chest with a water balloon. Al, who had just lost his two front teeth, stood grinning like a jack-o-lantern at the bottom of the stairs. "I'm gonna get you," I yelled then raced down the stairs after him.

Al ran around the back of the house giving me enough time to open the faucet on the sprinklers. I heard Kayla squeal with delight as water splashed around the yard.

"Don't tell me you started without me?" a voice called from the porch.

I turned to see Kate coming down the stairs, looking adorable in her red polka-dot bikini. It highlighted the red, heart-shaped beach glass pendant lying on her chest.

"Sorry." I called, turning to join her, pretending I didn't see Al sneaking up on me from the other side of the porch. "Everything okay?" I asked her, studying the worried expression on her face.

She shrugged. "More gray hairs," she said then, fluffing her long, blonde locks.

"That happens." I said, leaning in to kiss her cheek, "when you're human."

Before she could answer, however, Al launched his attack, drenching us both. This time, however, Kate ran after him. I watched her go, my wife, my savior, my...mermaid, who had given up her last spark of magic for me, not knowing the gift it would give her in return. I smiled as I watched her laugh, tickling our little boy until he crumpled to the ground, our daughter joining in the fun. My wife, whom I would grow old with and would love until the day I died...many years from now.

THANK YOU

I hope you enjoyed *The Glass Mermaid*. Let's keep in
touch! I occasionally send newsletters with cover
reveals and free flash fiction pieces. I also update my
readers when I have new releases and sales. Would
you like to join me, poppet? Go here to join:

http://eepurl.com/bbaeo9

Thanks so much for reading,

POPPY

ABOUT POPPY

Romance author. Cupcake connoisseur. Certified herbalist. Beach bum. Fan of all things Starbucks. Holistic healing advocate. Surfer girl wanna-be. Lost guru. Maker of dandelion wine. Counselor. Paranormal buff. Etsy addict. Secretly Jedi. So not a geek girl. Gifted in sarcasm. Hot wife. Ninja mom. And now, I'm ready to share a whole head full of witty, mouthy, smart, lovely, heart-warming, and hot characters with the world. Are you ready?

Poppy Lawless is the author of the *The Glass Mermaid* and the forthcoming novella. *The Cupcake Witch*. Poppy holds degrees in English and Psychology. She is a counselor in the field of mental health and is a trained herbalist. Poppy's new series blends the best of romance with a *Practical Magic* or contemporary *Bewitched* appeal.

Keep in touch with the author online.
www.poppylawless.com
https://www.facebook.com/authorpoppylawless
https://www.pinterest.com/lovepotionbooks/
https://twitter.com/ThePoppyLawless

ABOUT THE FALLING IN DEEP COLLECTION

From mermaids to sirens, Miami to Athens, dark paranormal romance to contemporary stories with steam, the fifteen award-winning and best-selling authors of *The Falling in Deep Collection* are bringing you mermaid tales like you've never seen before.

The Falling in Deep Collection

Scales by Pauline Creeden

Ink: A Mermaid Romance by Melanie Karsak

Of Ocean and Ash by A. R. Draeger

Deep Breath by J. M. Miller

At the Heart of the Deep by Carrie Wells

The Mermaid's Den by Ella Malone

The Water is Sweeter by Eli Constant

The Glass Mermaid by Poppy Lawless

An Officer & a Mermaid by Blaire Edens

How to be a Mermaid by Erin Hayes

Cold Water Bridegroom by B. Brumley

Before the Sea by Emily Goodwin

Immersed by Katie Hayoz

Siren's Kiss by Margo Bond Collins

To Each His Own by Anna Albergucci

CPSIA information can be obtained at www.ICGtesting.com
Printed in the USA
LVOW08s1925170516

488667LV00006BA/517/P

ML 5/16